© 2001 Grandreams Books Limited.
Published by Grandreams Books Ltd.
4 North Parade, Bath, BA1 1LF. UK

Grandreams, Inc.,
4 Crossroads Drive, Suite #108, Robbinsville, NJ 08691.USA

Printed in China

Snow White & the Seven Dwarfs

ILLUSTRATED BY DAVID LONG

Story adapted by
Christine Deverell

It was the middle of winter. A Queen sat by a window made of the finest black ebony. As she looked out at the snow, she pricked her finger and three drops of blood fell onto it. She gazed at the red drops in the white snow and said, "I wish my little daughter to be as white as the snow, as red as blood and as black as ebony ."

And her daughter was beautiful, with skin as white as snow, cheeks as rosy as the blood, and hair as black as ebony. Her name was Snow White. Sadly the Queen died, and Snow White's father married another wife. This Queen had a magic mirror. She would gaze at herself and say,

"Mirror, mirror, on the wall,

Who is the fairest of them all?"

And the mirror would reply,

"You, O Queen, are the fairest in the land."

7

One day, when she looked into the mirror, it answered her,

"You my Queen, may lovely be

But Snow White is by far

The most beautiful in the land."

The Queen called one of her servants and ordered him to take Snow White out into the woods. "I never want to see her again", she screeched! The servant was very unhappy and did not want to hurt Snow White. So he left her in the woods, and returned to the Queen to tell her that Snow White was gone forever. Poor Snow White was left alone to wander in the woods.

As night fell, she reached a cottage. It was the home of seven dwarfs. Inside, she found a table neatly laid with seven small loaves of bread and seven little glasses of wine.

Against the wall were seven small beds.

Snow White was very hungry, so she helped herself to a little bread from each loaf, and a sip of wine from each glass. Then she lay down and fell asleep.

When they returned from their day's work, the seven dwarfs were not at all pleased with the mess that they saw on the table. They turned around and found Snow White sleeping soundly.

At first they grumbled and complained to one another, but then, they all gazed in amazement at her beauty, and agreed to let her sleep until morning.

Snow White stayed with the dwarfs. While they were hard at work in the Diamond Mine, she looked after their cottage and prepared the meals every day.

One day, the Queen
looked into her mirror and
asked her usual question.

The mirror replied;
"You are the fairest
in this place.

But by far the most
beautiful face
Belongs to
Snow White."

The Queen was furious. "I thought she was dead!" she cried. She disguised herself as an old gypsy woman and went off into the woods in search of Snow White. She carried with her a basket of apples. One of the apples was poisoned on one side.

When she came upon the cottage, she knocked on the door. Snow White opened the window, looked out and said,

"I dare not let anyone in."

"Never mind dear. Just let me give you one of my beautiful apples."

Snow White did not want to take it, but the Queen said,

"Look, I will take a bite of this apple and you will see that it is safe."

Snow White then took a bite of the apple and fell down on the ground.

15

When the dwarfs returned from work that day they were very unhappy to find Snow White lying on the ground. She was so beautiful and they wanted to look at her forever, so they laid her in a glass case.

Snow White looked as if she were only sleeping. One day a prince rode by and begged the dwarfs to let him take Snow White away with him. They refused at first, but then they took pity on him, and granted his wish.

As soon as he lifted the glass cover, a piece of apple fell from Snow White's lips, and she awoke. The Prince asked Snow White to go with him to his father's palace and marry him.

Snow White and the Prince reigned happily over that land for many, many years.